Dion Bourcicault

Jessie Brown

SALZWASSER
VERLAG

Dion Bourcicault

Jessie Brown

Reprint of the original, first published in 1859.

1st Edition 2022　|　ISBN: 978-3-37513-112-8

Verlag (Publisher): Salzwasser Verlag GmbH, Zeilweg 44, 60439 Frankfurt, Deutschland
Vertretungsberechtigt (Authorized to represent): E. Roepke, Zeilweg 44, 60439 Frankfurt, Deutschland
Druck (Print): Books on Demand GmbH, In de Tarpen 42, 22848 Norderstedt, Deutschland

BOURCICAULT'S DRAMATIC WORKS.

No. 6.

JESSIE BROWN;

OR,

THE RELIEF OF LUCKNOW.

A Drama, in Three Acts.

BY DION BOURCICAULT.

TO WHICH ARE ADDED

A description of the Costume—Cast of the Characters—Entrances and Exits—
Relative Positions of the Performers on the Stage, and the whole of the
Stage Business.

This Play forms No. 203 of French's Edition of the Standard Drama.

NEW YORK:

SAMUEL FRENCH

No. 122 Nassau Street, Up Stairs.

Boucicault's Dramatic Works.

FORMING THE REPERTOIRE OF

MISS AGNES ROBERTSON.

No. VI.

JESSIE BROWN;

OR,

THE RELIEF OF LUCKNOW.

A Drama, in Three Acts.

(FOUNDED ON AN EPISODE IN THE INDIAN REBELLION.)

BY

Dion Boucicault;

AUTHOR OF

London Assurance, Old Heads and Young Hearts, The Irish Heiress, Used Up, The
Corsican Brothers, Love and Money, The Willow Copse, The Life of an Actress,
The Phantom, Andy Blake, The Chameleon, Victor and Hortense, Genevieve,
The Young Actress, Louis the Eleventh, The Knight of Arva, Faust and
Marguerite, Janet Pride, George D'Arville, The Poor of New York,
Belphegor, Napoleon's Old Guard, Love in a Maze, Alma Mater,
A Lover by Proxy, Don Cæsar de Bazan, The Invisible
Husband, Sixtus the Fifth, The Prima Donna, Bluebelle,
The Cat Changed into a Woman, Una, The Fox
Hunt, &c., &c., &c.

NEW YORK:

SAMUEL FRENCH,

122 NASSAU STREET, (UP STAIRS.)

CAST OF CHARACTERS.—[JESSIE BROWN.]

Wallack's Theatre, 1858.

THE NANA SAHIB, Rajah of Bithoor, -	Mr. Bourcicault.
ACHMET, his Vakeel, - - - - -	Mr. H. B. Phillips.
RANDAL MCGREGOR, } Officers in the Eng-	Mr. Lester.
GEORDIE MCGREGOR, } lish Service,	Mr. A. H. Davenport.
REV. DAVID BLOUNT, Chaplain 32nd Regiment,	Mr. W. R. Blake.
SWEENIE, a Private, 32d Regiment, - -	Mr. T. B. Johnston.
CASSIDY, a Corporal, 32d Regiment, -	Mr. Sloan.

Soldiers, Highlanders, Sepoys, and Hindoo Servants.

JESSIE BROWN, a Scotch Girl, - - -	Miss Agnes Robertson.
AMY CAMPBELL, - - - - - -	Mrs. Hoey.
CHARLIE and EFFIE, her Children, - -	Misses Reeves.
ALICE, - - - - - - -	Mrs. Allen.
MARY, - - - - - - -	Mrs. H. B. Phillips.

Ladies and Children.

The Scene is laid at Lucknow, in the Province of Oude, in India.

Time—The Summer of 1857.

JESSIE BROWN.

ACT I.

SCENE I.—*The Exterior of the Bungalo of Mrs. Campbell—Lucknow in the distance. Table laid on* R. H. *side, under a tree, with viands upon it. Native servants in attendance.*

MUSIC.—*Enter* GEORDIE McGREGOR, *with* ALICE *and* MARY. *Enter* ACHMET *from the house.*

Geor. Here we are at last. What can induce Mrs. Campbell to live a mile from Lucknow ?

Alice. You are a pretty soldier—you cannot march a mile without a murmur.

Geor. On my own native hills in bonnie Scotland, with my hound by my side, I have walked a dozen miles before breakfast ; but under this Indian sun——

Mary. And with only a pretty girl by your side——

Alice. Say two pretty girls. Don't be bashful, Mary—include me.

Enter MRS. CAMPBELL.

Geor. Oh, Mrs. Campbell, look here ! I am besieged—Delhi is nothing to the condition I shall be in if you don't relieve me.

Alice. Mrs. Campbell, please, he won't tell us which of us he is in love with.

Mrs. C. I will tell you: with neither. He is in love with his new uniform ; he only received his commission two months ago, and every officer is for six months in love with himself.

Geor. After that I'll take a glass of sangaree.

Mrs. C. Where's Randal ?

Geor. My fiery brother, the McGregor—as Jessie will insist on call‑ing him—is, as usual, inspecting his men.

Mrs. C. Jessie is right; for your brother, Randal McGregor, is the noblest man that ever breathed the Scottish air and made it purer. But tell me, what news from Delhi? [*They sit.*

Geor. Oh, the siege continues; but it will be taken, of course—these black rascals are mere scum.

[ACHMET, *who is serving* GEORDIE, *looks round.*

Alice. There is one who disagrees with you on that point.

Geor. Does he?

Ach. No, sahib, Allah Akbar! it is so—we are scum. Lady, in Hindoostan there are one hundred millions such as I am, and there are one hundred thousand such as you; yet for a century you have had your foot on our necks; we are to you a thousand to one—a thousand black necks to one white foot. God is just, and Moham‑med is his prophet. We are scum!

Geor. I can't answer for the truth of your calculation, but I agree in the sentiment—you are scum. [*Drinks.*

Ach. Sometimes the scum rises.

Geor. Yes, Dusky, and when it does, the pot boils over and puts the fire out; so the scum extinguishes the element that made it rise.

Ach. I cannot reason with a European.

Geor. No, nor fight with one; by your own calculation it takes one thousand of you to do either one or the other. [*Exit* ACHMET.

Mrs. C. Beware of that man, Geordie; I did not like the expression of his face as you spoke.

Geor. Bah! there is virtue enough in one red-coat to put a whole army of them to flight.

Mrs. C. Have you ever been in battle?

Geor. Never. But when I'm on parade, and hear the drums and see the uniforms, I feel like the very devil.

Alice. There is no chance of the war coming here—is there?

Geor. Not the slightest. London itself is not more peaceable than yonder city of Lucknow; the native regiments here are faithful as dogs. You need not fear danger.

Mrs. C. The rebellion is still far. But when I think of the atrocities already perpetrated by the Sepoys—when I think of my two little children—oh, why do I remain here in the midst of such scenes of horror?

Geor. Because you are in love with my brother Randal; the feel‑ings of the mother urge you to go and the feelings of the woman com‑mand you to stay'

Mrs. C. [*Rising.*] Geordie, there is more truth than kindness in what you say.

Geor. [*Holds her.*] Stay, Amy, I'm a thoughtless fool.

Mrs. C. Yet you wrong me a little—I was betrothed to Randal. We quarreled, as lovers will, and parted. In that moment of anger I accepted the hand of Colonel Campbell.

Geor. At the seige of Sebastopol Randal became your husband's most devoted friend, and watched over him like a brother.

Mrs. C. Oh! it was a noble reproof to my falsehood.

Geor. And at the charge of the Highlanders, when Campbell was struck down mortally wounded, and the command devolved on my brother, Randal carried him in his arms, at the head of the regiment, into the Redan, so that none of the glory of that day should be lost to his rival.

Mrs. C. Should I not be unfaithful to my dead husband if I did not love Randal McGregor as I do?

[*Jessie, outside, sings.*

Mary. Hush, listen! [*Geordie goes up.*

Alice. What is that?

Geordie. What is it? why it is a sprig of heather from the High-land moors. It is a slogan on the Scotch pipes that nature has put into the prettiest throat that ever had an arm round it. It is the pet of the regiment. It is Jessie Brown.

Mrs. C. Yes, 'tis Jessie, here she comes up the hill with her two lovers.

Alice. Two lovers! That's extra allowance.

Geor. She might have eight hundred if she liked, for that is the strength of the 78th Regiment, and there's not a man in it that would not stake his life for a blink of her blue eye.

Mrs. C. Jessie is a good girl, as honest and true as steel. She is betrothed to Sweenie Jones, a private in the 32d.

Geor. An ugly, wiry little fellow, but a smart soldier and as brave as a terrier.

Mrs. C. But she is also followed by a soft, good-natured Irish cor-poral named Cassidy, the bosom friend of Sweenie, and to see these two men so devoted to each other, and yet so fond of the same girl, is a picture too like my own history not to fill me with interest and emotion. [*Music.—Scotch air—very piano.*

Geor. She belongs to our clan.

Alice. Here she comes.

Mrs. C. And here come my darling ones.

Enter SWEENIE, *carrying* CHARLIE *on his back, and* CASSIDY *carrying* EFFIE *on his shoulder.*

Char. Wo, hossey! come up. [SWEENIE *tries to salute* GEORDIE. CASSIDY *salutes him.*

Effie. [*Beating* CASSIDY *with her parasol.*] Go along, hossy.

Char. Oh, Sweenie, you'll have me down, hold me up, sir.

Enter JESSIE.*—Music ceases.*

Jessie. Dinna ye hear the bairn, ye lout, hau'd him up.

Sween. How can I when I must salute my officer?

Jessie. Ee, sirs, its maister Geordie—gude day, leddies—ee, ma certie, how braw a chiel he is in his red coat, and his gou'd lace. There's McGregor in every inch of him. Ee why wasn't I the Queen of Scotland to make a king of him.

Geor. Don't be a fool, Jessie, you talk just as you did when we were children.

Jessie. And wha shouldn't I, Geordie, then, in the days of auld lang syne, when we played together on the craigs o' Duncleuch, you aye used to kiss me when we met and parted—you do so now when there is nane to see—are you ashamed of those days when we were children, Geordie? I'm not.

Geor. No, Jessie, and I'll kiss you now if Sweenie does not mind.

Sween. No, your honor, if Jessie says all right, so it is.

Cas. We give our consint.

Alice. [*Vexed.*] Jessie has three lovers instead of two, it seems.

Jes. Eh! [*Aside.*] Yon lassie loo's him, I spier it in the blink o' her e'e. She is fashed wi' him for kissin' me.

Geor. [*Aside.*] Alice is furious. [*Aloud.*] Come, Jessie, for auld lang syne.

Jes. [*Snatching* CHARLIE *from* SWEENIE—*aside to* SWEENIE.] Say ye nae like it.

Sween. [*Puzzled.*] Eh,—What! Hold your honor; I ax pardon, but——

Jes. Sweenie's jealous.

Cas. We are chokin' wid it, plase your honor.

Mrs. C. [*who with* MARY *has watched this scene, and understood Jessie's motives, advances.*] Go along, all of you, take your sweethearts into the kitchen. Jessie, leave the children here.

Jes. 'Tention 32nd! fa' in. Recht fess.—March!

[*Exit Sweenie and Cassidy, following her word of command.*]

Mrs. C. [*Laughing.*] There girls, there's a pair of lovers reduced to discipline!

Alice. Yet people say that now-a-days the chivalry has left the Officers and is to be found in the ranks.

Mrs. C. No, Alice—Jessie is beloved, because all men worship what is brave, gentle, and good, because she shrinks from hurting another's feelings, even in jest, as she did yours just now.

Jes. Nae, my leddy—I knaw nout o' what yer spierin at.

Mrs. C. Then take that blush away.

[JESSIE *runs out, stops and returns timidly to* ALICE.

Jes. [*in a low voice.*] Ye are nae angry wi' puir Jessie.

Alice. [*Turns and throws her arms round her neck and kisses her.*] No. [*Jessie runs off.*

Mrs. C. Now, Geordie, you can take Jessie's kiss where she has left it, and I am sure you will hurt nobody's feelings.

Alice. Oh, Amy. [*Geordie crosses to Alice.*

Mrs. C. Come girls, take Geordie in, I would be alone.

[*Music, exit* GEORDIE, ALICE *and* MARY.

Mrs. C. Randal is coming, I cannot hear his footstep, but it falls on my heart, he is beyond my senses, but love, that heavenly essence, gives me a feeling finer than sense, and I know that my lover comes. 'Tis the air he breathes, that conveys his presence to me, as it flutters through my heart.

Enter RANDAL MCGREGOR.

Ran. Amy.

Mrs. C. Ah, I knew it.

Char. Oh, dere's Randal.

Effie. No, Charlie, me first, kiss Effie first. [*They run to him.*

Ran. There, that will do, run along, go Charlie, go Effie, you tease me. [*The Children shrink back.*

Mrs. C. Come away dears, you are tired, Randal.

Ran. No, but the sight of those children pains me.

Mrs. C. They remind you that I have been unfaithful—oh Randal, do not visit the fault of the mother upon these innocent children.

Ran. Amy, your repentance wounds me, and your memory of that fault is a reproach to my love. Oh, let it be buried in the grave of your noble husband.

Mrs. C. Forgive me.

Ran. Charlie, come here, Effie, come. [*He kisses them.*] Amy, I have bad news, the rebels are at Cawnpore, not fifty miles from hence, and a report has just arrived, that tells of horrors committed on our countrymen, their wives, their children, that makes my blood freeze and my heart groan.

Mrs. C. Randal, Randal, are we in danger here, my children, are they safe.

Ran. Hush, one cry of alarm, one look of fear, and we are lost. Of our regiments in Lucknow, four will mutiny, one only will remain faithful, to-night you must leave this place.

Mrs. C. Is peril so near.

Enter two native servants, who remove the service.

Ran. Hush. {*Sings as he dances,* CHARLIE.

There is nae luck aboot the hoose.

There is nae luck at all, &c.

[*Mrs. Campbell leans, trembling, over the child at her side.* *Exeunt Natives.*

Mrs. C. They are gone.

Ran. Regain your courage, think of these children.

Mrs. C. Randal, you exagerate the danger; look around you—all is at peace, the people are kind and gentle—not a look of anger or of hate in any face; our servants are devoted to us.

Ran. Fatal security! Yonder country to you seems in repose—to me it seems like a sleeping tiger. Death is humming in the air. You say your servants are faithful—there is one of them watching us now—we are watched—don't turn—a tall black fellow in a crimson turban.

Mrs. C. Achmet.

Ran. Listen, without betraying any emotion. At midnight I shall bring down 50 men—be ready to start without delay; take nothing with you—make no preparation.

Mrs. C. Why cannot we fly now, at once?

Ran. Because your own servants would assassinate you, and join the army. [*Night begins.*

Mrs. C. May they not do so ere to-night.

Ran. No; I gave Cassidy and Sweenie leave to come here, and sent Geordie on—that makes three, and you have only 30 servants; the natives dare not attack at such odds.

Mrs. C. Does Geordie know our peril?

Ran. No; nor is it necessary, until the hour arrives. He is young, and might lack coolness.

Mrs. C. Why do you suspect my household of treachery?

Ran. [*Drawing out a paper.*] Do you know the Rajah of Bithoor?

Mrs. C. Nana Sahib—I saw him at Benares, at the feast of Mohammedah, a year ago. I might not have recollected him, but he followed me with so a strange gaze that he almost terrified me.

Ran. Do you understand Hindoostanee?

Mrs. C. No.

Ran. I do. [*As he reads,* ACHMET *glides on behind, and creeps to his shoulder.*] This letter was intercepted at Secunderah, to-day. Listen as I translate : "My faithful Achmet—to-night, at one hour after the set of moon, I shall be at the Martiniere with 500 men ; when the Feringhee woman is in my Zenana, to you I give a lac of rupees. Destroy the children—they are giaours. Nana Sahib."

[ACHMET *raises a knife over* RANDAL.

Mrs. C. My children! [*Music. Sees* ACHMET *and utters a cry;* ACHMET *drops his knife, runs up and leaps over the parapet.* RANDAL *turns, draws a pistol and fires at him as he disappears.*

Re-enter GEORDIE, ALICE, MARY, JESSIE, SWEENIE, *and* CASSIDY.

Ran. Do not be alarmed. 'Twas only—a jackal ; I fired and scared him away.

Cas. A jackal is it—then, be jabers, here he comes back again—and on his hind legs.

Enter BLOUNT, *with his hat smashed.*

All. Mr. Blount !

Ran. The Chaplain of our Regiment.

Cas. His Riverence !

Blount. Good evening, my friends. May I suggest that the next time you throw a fellow six foot high out of an upper window, you would intimate your views to peaceable persons below.

Cas. A jackal, six foot high !

Geor. Are you hurt, sir?

Blount. No ; fortunately I received the thing on my head—from whence it bounded off, and rolled down the hill-side into the jungle.

Ran. Return to the house, all of you. [*Exeunt all but* MRS. CAMPBELL. Mr. Blount, stay ! one word—you are a clergyman—but once you were, I believe, an officer in Her Majesty's Carbineers.

Blount. I quitted the army from conscientious scruples.

Ran. Are you a coward ?

Blount. A coward! I think not—that is—well—no ; for when I read the accounts of these atrocities, I feel in me an emotion that is evil, very evil—a sinful desire to smash the heads of these wretches, who butcher women and infants. I know the feeling is horrible ; I ought to forgive and pray for them. I have bound the devil in me, but he leaks out.

Ran. If you saw these little ones in peril, would you fight?

Blount. Fight! young man—my dear Randal—I kill human beings! a clergyman destroy lives! what do you take me for?

Ran. I take you for a brave man. You were born a warrior, but your more gentle nature refused to war against any creatures but the wicked, and you could not shed blood except in the cause of humanity. Don't deny it; you retired from the army and became curate of a poor Scotch village near my home; from your lips I first learned what war was.

Blount. I portrayed its horrors, its wickedness.

Ran. I only saw its glory; I only saw your face lighted with the animation of the charge—you fired my soul and made me what I am—

Blount. God forgive me; I ruined the boy.

Ran. I entered the army—you followed me.

Blount. Did I not promise your dying father to watch over you? and here's how I did it.

Ran. Listen, my dear old tutor. You are brave and cool, and to you alone I can confide the defence of this house to-night.

Blount. To me—good gracious!

Ran. You will be surrounded by Nana Sahib's troops; his design is to murder all its inmates except Amy, whom he destines for his Zenana.

Blount. The demon! May his infernal spirit roast in—what am I saying! May a merciful Father forgive him! This is horrible.

Ran. At midnight summon all the household, and start for the city. I will precede you and gather a guard, and hasten back to meet you.

Mrs. C. Do you go alone?

Ran. My horse is at the foot of the hill, picketed in the copse; once on his back, I am in Lucknow. Farewell.
[*Music. Embraces* MRS. C.

Mrs. C. Oh, Randal, shall we ever meet again?

Ran. We sleep to-night in yonder city or in Heaven. [*Exit* RANDAL.

Blount. Stop, Randal, my dear boy; I can't do it. He is gone— what shall I do? Mercy on me! what arms are there in the house?

Mrs. C. Two double guns, a rifle, my late husband's swords and a brace of pistols.

Blount. A clergyman—a minister of peace—what will become of me! Have you any powder?

Mrs. C. A small keg of cartridges?

Blount. These poor children! I tremble in every limb. Have you any caps?

Mrs. C. A box or two.

Blount. The old devil is kicking in me—my blood beats hot. Get thee behind me, Satan! Oh! if I could only see these deluded murderers, to speak with them, to prepare their erring souls, before I sent them to ask for that mercy in Heaven which, by the way, they never show on earth. [*Music.*] My respected and dear friend, we are engaged in a wicked deed—I feel it—come, let us see your ammunition.
[*Exeunt.*

SCENE II.—*A verandah attached to the house. Night.*

Enter SWEENIE *and* CASSIDY.

Cas. Whisht! Sweenie, come here—spake low! D'ye see that
wood beyant ? there's fifty black divils hidin' in it, and here's one of
their raping hooks I found in the grass.

Sween. Rebels here !

Cas. I was watchin' the Capting ; as he hurried down they crept
afther him. He has come to grief, Sweenie, for yonder is the road
to Lucknow, and his horse has not passed down it yet. Oh, wurra,
wurra, what will we do?

Sween. Give me that sabre; stop here, Cassidy, I will creep down
and see what is going on below ; don't say a word to frighten the
women, but if I don't come back in ten minutes, conclude I'm dead ;
then, in with ye, barricade the doors, and tell Master Geordie.

Cas. Sweenie, avich, let me go. Oh, murdher! you'll be killed
and Jessie wil never forgive me for not goin' in your place.

Sween. Cassidy, if the rebels are here in force, I shall fall ; and as
the savage spare neither women nor children, I'll see ye both in
Heaven before morning, so I won't say good night.   [*Exit.*

Cas. God speed ye, Sweenie, an keep ye.

Enter JESSIE.

Jes. Who is that? Cassidy !

Cas. Meself, darlin'.   [*Distant shot.*

Jes. What s that !

Cas. [*Aside.*] Its murdherin' the Captain they are, I dar'nt tell
her. [*Aloud*] That, that was Sweenie, sure he's gone down beyant,
may be, that is by accident, his swoord went off on half cock.

Jes. His sword !

Enter GEORDIE.

Geor. Jessie, come here; eh, who's that—Cassidy?

Cas. [*Aside.*] What'll I do at all, if if he knew that Sweenie was
gone to get killed for his brother.

Geor. Go in, Cassidy, leave us.

Cas. I'm off, your honor. [*Going.*] Five minutes are gone, I'll creep
afther Sweenie. If I had a bagginit, or a taste ov a twig itself, but
I've nothin' in my hand but my fist.   [*Exit.*

Jes. Did ye ca' me.

Geor. Come here, you little puss, now you shall give me that kiss
I did not get this afternoon.

Jes. Geordie you have been drinking.

Geor. And if I have. Wine lets out the truth, Jessie, and the truth
is—I love you.

Jes. Ee ! dinna ye always loov me ?

Geor. No, I love you as you deserve to be loved, and I can't bear
to see such a pretty girl as you have grown throw yourself away on
those common soldiers, like Sweenie and his comrades.

Jes. Oh, Geordie, Sweenie loves you—he would die for you or
Randal

Geor. Oh, devil take Sweenie! all our mess say you are too good for him. You are the prettiest girl in Lucknow.

Jes. Let us gang awa in, Geordie dear.

Geor. [*Taking her in his arms.*] No, you sha'n't—come, don't be foolish, Jessie. Could you not be happy with me—don't you like an officer better than a vulgar, common soldier.

Jes. Oh, Geordie! oh, Geordie!   [*Buries her face in her hands.*

Geor. Look up, Jessie.

Jes. I canna, I canna.

Geor. Why can't you look up into my face?

Jes. I'm lukin far awa—far awa, upon craigs of Duncleuch; 'tis in the days of auld lang syne, and the arm of wee Geordie McGregor is round the body of Jessie Brown, for he is saving her life in the sea. Na, don't tak yer arm awa, Geordie dear. I'm lukin still. Geordie is a laddie noo, and he chases the deer on the craigs of Duncleuch; beside him is poor Sweenie—poor faithful Sweenie, that follows the McGregor like a dog; Geordie drives a stag to bay; the beastie rushes on him and throws him doon— anither minit and Geordie will na see Jessie mair—but Sweenie's dirk is quicker than that minit! the brute fell dead, but not before he gored poor Sweenie sorely. We watched by his bedside; d'ye mind the time, Geordie? your arm was round me then—na, dinna tak it awa noo.

Geor. Oh, Jessie! oh, Jessie!

Jes. Luk up, Geordie.

Geor. I cannot.

Jes. Why canna ye luk up into my face?

Geor. Because I'm looking far away, far away into the days of auld lang syne, and they make me ashamed of what I am.

Jes. The bluid of shame never crossed the brow of a McGregor, Na! na! you may kiss me now; but listen, Geordie; whisper—
        [*Sings.*

> Should auld acquaintance be forgot
> And never brought to mind,
> Should auld acquaintance be forgot
> And the days of auld lang syne.
> For auld lang syne, my dear,
> For auld lang syne,
> Then tak a kiss of kindness yet
> For auld lang syne.   [*Exeunt.*

SCENE III.—*The Interior of the Bungalo. A room serving for a nursery —large openings at the back discover a distant view of Lucknow, brilliant with lights.*

MRS. CAMPBELL *discovered.* CHARLIE *and* EFFIE, ALICE *and* MARY.

Mrs. C. No, I shall not undress the children. Take Effie with you, Alice.

Alice. Poor child, she is almost asleep now.

Char. Mamma, I want to go to bed. Where is Jessie?

Enter JESSIE.

Jes. Here, my precious one. [*Exit* ALICE *and* MARY, *with* EFFIE.
Mrs. C. Place him in his cot ; do not remove his clothes. [*Walks
up and down. Aside.*] I have calmed the agitation of the poor old
chaplain, but my own overpowers me.

Char. Jessie, sing me Charlie ; you are not tired, are you ?

Jes. Nae, darling ; I'm never tired o' teaching ye the airs o' Scotland.   [*Sings a verse of "Charlie is my Darling."*
     Mrs. C. Can I entrust the secret to this girl ? [*Aloud.*] Jessie !

Jes. Aweel, my lady.

Mrs. C. There's danger near. Don't start, don't cry. To-night
this house is to be surrounded by the rebels—our murder is planned,
but so is our escape.

Jes. [*Rising.*] It canna be ; wha tauld ye this?

Mrs. C. Randal McGregor.

Jes. Then it's true.

Mrs. C. Hush ! five hundred men will attack us:

Jes. Mercy on us! what will become of us ?

Mrs. C. Randal has promised to rescue us.

Jes. [*Resuming her calmness.*] The McGregor has said it ; dinna ye
fash yersel—gin he said it, he'll do it.   [*Returns to the cot.*

Mrs. C. Go, Jessie, see to the fastenings of all the doors, but show
no fear, excite no suspicion.

Jessie. I hae no fear. Has not the McGregor gi'en his word to coom
back ? He'l tak it up, and under his claymore there can nae fear.
                              [*Exit hastily.—Music.*

Mrs. C. This girl gives me a lesson in courage—what reliance,
what noble confidence she has in Randal—how calm she turned,
when she heard he had given his word to secure our escape.

[NANA SAHIB *and* ACHMET *appear at the window, on the balcony.* ACHMET
points to MRS. CAMPBELL. *The* NANA *enters the chamber.* ACHMET *disappears.*

What is the hour ? [*Goes up and looks at her watch.*] It is now past
eleven. Randal must have reached the city by this time—it is time
to prepare. [*She turns and sees the* NANA *beside her.*] Mercy !

Nana. Be silent—you know me.

Mrs. C. The Nana Sahib.

Nana. The officer who intercepted my letter to Achmet, is my
prisoner. My men are now surrounding your park. Escape is hope-
less.

Mrs. C. [*Aside.*] Randal taken prisoner ! then we are lost.

Nana. Listen! I saw you at Benares—your soul entered through my
eyes into my heart, and thrust out my own. I followed you, until
like the sun you passed away where I could follow no more ; I went
to Bithoor, and my wives offended your soul in me. I gave them
riches and sent them away—my Zenana is cold—I am there alone ; it
awaits the form to which the soul here belongs.

Mrs. C. You would murder my children and dishonor their mother.

Nana. Your children shall be mine, princes of the Mahratta ; follow me and no blood shall flow. I will withdraw my men. Lucknow shall be spared, and peace restored.

Mrs. C. England would spurn the peace bought thus with the honor of one of her people.

Nana. [*Approaching the bed.*] This is your child?

Mrs. C. My child.

Nana. [*Draws his yataghan.*] No cry ! or this steel is in his throat !

Char. Mamma, oh, dear mamma, help me.

Mrs. C. Hush, Charlie, my own one, don't cry, hush. Oh, Rajah Sahib, spare my child ; yes, I consent.

Enter JESSIE.

I will follow you—spare—

[JESSIE *snatches the knife from the* NANA, *and stabbing him with it suddenly.*

Jes. Drop that bairn, ye black deevil ! [NANA *staggers a moment and drops the child, whom* JESSIE *catches to her breast.*

Nana. Tehanum possess ye—mine then ye shall be by force—none under this roof but you, shall see to-morrow's sun.

[*Distant shots—cries within—*ACHMET *appears.* NANA *and* ACHMET *draw their scimeters and leap over the balcony.*

Enter GEORDIE, ALICE, *and* MARY.

Geor. What shots were those?

Alice. What has happened?

Mrs. C. The Nana Sahib with five hundred rebels, besiege us in this house. Randal is their prisoner. Randal who promised to rescue us.

Jes. Prisoner or free, the McGregor will keep his word.

Mrs. C. The impassibility of that girl drives me mad.

Enter CASSIDY, *running.*

Cas. He's comin' thunder and turf, he's fightin' like a cat wid tin legs and fifteen claws on aich fut.

Alice. Who?

Cas. The Captain ; Sweenie is fightin' beside him. [*Shots outside.*] Hurroo ! they're at it.

[*Runs up,* GEORDIE *follows to verandah at back.*

Geor. There they are in the copse.

Cas. Where's a gun, oh a gun for the love o' God.

Jes. Here is one. [*Shots.*

Cas. Hoo ! there goes a bullet through my leg. [GEORDIE *staggers back very pale.* JESSIE *runs up with the gun.*] The devils see us in the light here, and they're pepperin' us handsome.

Jes. Look, Cassidy, look ! there's a big fellow makin' for Sweenie, quick. [CASSIDY *fires.*

Cas. Hoo !

Jes. Here they come—quick by this ladder.

Enter SWEENIE, *and then* RANDAL. JESSIE *comes down and soothe⁸*
        CHARLIE *and* EFFIE.

Ran. Cast down that ladder, Cassidy, and stand to your arms.
Cas. Ay, your honor.
Mrs. C. Oh, Randal, you have escaped!
Jes. I told you the McGregor would keep his word.
Ran. I was taken prisoner, by about fifty men, who lie just this
side of the bridge, their main force is still beyond the river, they are
led by some Rajah of rank.
Mrs. C. By the Nana Sahib in person, he was here.
Alice. Here!
Mrs. C. He came by that ladder, and fled when wounded by Jessie.
Jes. Na! the deevil had a steel jacket on, the blow slipped awa.
Ran. Nana Sahib, then the whole force of the rebels is in the
neighborhood—Lucknow is threatened—the garrison will be taken by
surprise, where is Geordie?
Geor. Here, Randal.   [*Advancing.*
Ran. How pale you are, are you wounded?
Geor. No—it is nothing.
Ran. A scratch I suppose. Geordie, a dispatch must be carried to
the city; I will write it, and you must bear it.
Mrs. C. But can Geordie escape thro' the lines of the enemy who
surround us. Death must be nearly certain.
Ran. Death is nearly certain, and therefore I pick my own brother
for the service; besides, he is an officer, and claims the post of dan-
ger as his right. Do you forget the name we bear? Alice, return
to the interior of the house. Come, Amy, give me paper and ink.
Geordie, while I am gone, see to your arms.
                 [*Exeunt all but* GEORDIE *and* JESSIE.
Geor. Death—he said that death is nearly certain.
Jes. How pale he is! Geordie, speak—are you hurt?
Geor. Oh, Jessie!
Jes. I saw ye flench from the shots—you came back white as snaw.
You tremble—what is it, Geordie dear?—tell me.
Geor. I can't, Jessie. My tongue fails me—as my limbs do—oh,
Jessie—I feel I cannot face the fire.
Jes. What say ye?
Geor. I am a coward.   [*Falls in a chair.*
Jes. Na! [*Runs to him.*] Hush, dearie; there's nae drop of coward
bluid in the McGregor—tak' time, Geordie.
Geor. I cannot help it, Jessie; the passion of fear is on me—I can-
not stir.
Jes. Oh, my heart! oh, my heart! My Geordie, think of what
Randal will say if he sees ye so—his ain brither—his ainly one!
Think, dearie, there are women here—and bairns, puir helpless things
—and if ye flench noo, they will be killed!
Geor. I know it—[*hides his face and his hands*]—but I am paralyzed.
Jes. Think of the auld mither at hame, Geordie—the proud one that
nursed ye, Geordie—the leddy that awaits her twa boys cumin' back
fra' the wars—what! will ye bring yer mither back a blighted name?

Oh, hae courage, for her sake!—oh, for mine, Geordie! [*Throws her arms around him.*] Oh, why canna' I gang beside ye, to show ye how to bleed for the auld braes o' Scotland?

Enter BLOUNT.

Wha's there?—gang awa'—oh, 'tis the minister.

Blount. Is he wounded? my poor boy, is he hurt?

Jes. Oh, sir, help him; his heart fails—it is his first fight, and he flenches.

. *Geor.* This terrible sense of fear which paralyzes me will pass away. 'Tis a spasm—it cannot be that my father's son, my brother's brother, can be so miserable, so contemptible a thing as this!

Blount. The boy has conscientious scruples, like me.

Geor. No, no; to you—to you alone, companions of my childhood, let me confess—

Blount. No, don't; you sha'n't say a word—you don't understand; I know all—first powder smells sick; but after you see a few men fall, that goes off.

Jes. Yes, it clears awa'.

Blount. Take your lip between your teeth and choose your man.

Jes. Think o' the bairnes they've slaughtered in cauld bluid.

Blount. Don't trust to pistols—I always preferred steel, it's more reliable and doesn't miss fire; use the point—it kills ten when the blade throws open your guard, and only wounds one. God forgive me! I am teaching this boy how to murder.

Re-enter RANDAL, *with the order, followed by* SWEENIE.

Ran. Here is the dispatch. Where is my brother?

Jes. He is here, but stay a wee. [*Aside.*] Oh, what can we do?

Ran. How's this? what has happened?

Jes. Naething. [*Aside*] He blenches, he canna' do it. [*Aloud.*] Randal, I have asked Geordie a favor, and he has granted me. That order, winna' the soldier that bears it safe to the General get advancement?

Ran. My brother will win a brevet rank of lieutenant.

Jes. Na; your brither is rich and can buy his rank, but my Sweenie is puir, and Geordie has consented to let Sweenie tak' his place and win his sergeant's stripes.

Sween. Oh Master Geordie! do you so? God bless ye! there's not a prouder boy in the Queen's uniform to-night than I am!

Geor. Jessie! Jessie!

Jes. Dinna' speak.

Blount. [*Aside.*] She puts her own lover in the jaws of death! God bless her! God bless her!

Ran. It is better so—I have other work for Geordie. Quick then, Sweenie; at the copse, near the brook, my horse is tied to a tree. Can you ride?

Sween. I can hold on.

Ran. This letter to the General. I will defend this house till he comes to relieve us, or we are buried under its ruins. The alarm guns which will be fired from the fort when your news is known will apprise us that you are safe in Lucknow, and have escaped. We can both see the flash and hear them from here. Away with you..

Jes. God be wi' ye, Sweenie. God be wi' ye laddie.

[*Throws her arms round him.*

Sween. I'll deserve ye this time, Jessie ; ye'll be proud of me, dead or alive. [*Goes up.* JESSIE *falls on her knees.*

Blount. What are you about ? you are not going by that road, you will be seen.

Sween. I know it—they'll fire—'tis ten to one they'll miss me ; but I'll fall into the garden as if I was shot, and while they are thinking' me stiff, I'll be creepin' down to the horse and off to Lucknow.

Ran. Well, let me see you try it.

Jes. Oh ! my loov ! 'tis for Geordie's sake.

[RANDAL *and* SWEENIE *go into the balcony.*

Mrs. C. But why should Randal go ?

Blount. To lead his man, habit.

·[*A shot.* SWEENIE *falls over.—A cry from* JESSIE.

Ran. [*After watching, returns.*] 'Tis all right, he has escaped.

Jes. But he may be wounded ?

Ran. I think not, unless there were two bullets. I have got one here. [*Takes off his cap—his temple is bloody.*

Mrs. C. Randal !

Ran. Tut ! we have other things to do. [*Draws out a handkerchief, presses his forehead ; and replaces his cap.*] Now, Amy, to work, there are but three of us here, Geordie, Cassidy, and I.

Blount. You may say four ! I will lay aside my conscientious scruples, and like my namesake, David, I will strike the Philistines.

Ran. You have three native servants, who, I think may be trusted. There are not more than fifty Sepoys on this side of the bridge—now if we can destroy that bridge, we shall divide our foes and hold our own or a few hours.

Blount. There's a keg of powder down stairs, I'll take it down under my arm, and blow up the bridge. This enterprise is bloodless, it suits me exactly.

Ran. You propose with your form to creep down unobserved, you would be cut to pieces.

Blount. But if the piece of me that held the keg got there, I might accomplish the good deed. [*Aside.*] I'm afraid he will send Geordie.

Ran. Geordie, quick, you and I will see to this.

Geor I am ready. [*Rises.* RANDAL *embraces* AMY.

Jes. He's ganging, look, look, he goes bravely, the McGregor bluid is in his cheek, the dark fire is lechted.

Geor. Bless you, Jessie. [*Aside to her.*] Sweenie has not been sacrificed in vain. I'll not belie your love, Jessie, farewell.

[*Exit* GEORDIE *and* RANDAL.

Jes. He's gane, he's gane, baith gane—and Sweenie—and my courage has gane too.

Enter ALICE, MARY, *and the children.*

Alice. All is quiet.

Blount. That's a bad sign. But let us extinguish the lights, they serve the enemy.   [*He puts out the candle. Stage dark.*]

Mrs. C. Oh, Heaven protect us in this dark hour of peril, preserve my poor little children.

Blount. Amen?—they come! I see white figures in the garden.

Jes. My Sweenie, have they killed my poor Sweenie, oh this suspense is worse than death.

Blount. The house is surrounded, the whole collection is here.

Mrs. C. Cassidy, fire, why don't you fire on them.

Cas. [*Looking in.*] Plase yer honor ma'am, them savages is like birds—firin' frightens frightens them away, and if we coax them here awhile, sure they won't be seeing afther the Captain Randal.

Blount. Good heart, noble heart, oh Merciful Father in Heaven, it is a pity such good people should die. Have pity on us, have pity on these weak ones, and upon these little ones.

Jes. Oh! protect my puir Sweenie; don't let his bluid lie on my hands—don't break puir Jessie's heart. [*A distant explosion. Music.*]

Cas. [*Entering.*] D'ye hear that? It's the bridge! the devils are skelping back again to see what kind of hell is behind 'em.

     [*Sounds of conflict.*]

Blount. They are coming! I hear Randal's voice.

Ran. Cassidy! Cassidy!

Cas. That's me! here I am, your honor. Hoo!

     [*Leaps over the balcony and disappears.*]

Blount. The door, the door is fast inside.   [*Runs out, R. H.*

Jes. No alarm guns from the city! the time is passed; no sign that he has escaped, and I sent him, I sent him. Oh, Sweenie, Sweenie!

Mrs. C. They come—they are safe.

Enter RANDAL, *bearing* GEORDIE *in his arms.*

Ran. See to the doors.

Alice. He is dead!

Jes. Dead! wha's dead? [*Sees* GEORDIE, *and utters a scream of grief and horror.*] Geordie, what have ye done? ye have killed the bairn. Stand awa, a' o' ye. Geordie, Geordie, look to me. Oh! I did it—I killed him—only for me he wad nae have gane. Geordie! [*She kisses his face.*] Speak to me, dear! Oh, I shall go mad, Geordie, if ye dae not answer me—if ye do not luk to me. [GEORDIE *raises himself at this moment. A flash of a gun is seen from the distant city.*

Ran. Ha! the alarm gun from the city.   [*A second gun is heard.*

Geor. Jessie, Jessie, do you hear those guns? Sweenie has escaped, and after a', Geordie is not a coward.   [*He faints.*

END OF ACT I.

ACT II.

SCENE I.—*The interior of a Hindoo Temple in Lucknow.* JESSIE *chained,* L. H., *to a pillar.* GEORDIE *is lying on a pallet,* R. H., *chained also. Hindoo Guards at the back.* ACHMET, R. C. *A Divan,* L. C. *Stage sombre. Music.*

Geor. [*Awaking.*] Where am I? Oh, these chains, those dark walls, those darker faces—I am a prisoner—why did I awake?

Jes. Geordie, dear, you are better now, the fever has left ye.

Geor. Jessie, are you there? come near me.

Jes. I can't, dearie, the savages have tied me like a dog to the wall.

Geor. What place is this?

Jes. It's a church where they worship the deevil.

Geor. How long have I been here.

Jes. For six lang weeks.

Geor. Does the Residency still hold out against the rebels?

Jes. I dinna ken. I have been here a' the time.

Geor. Were you taken prisoner when I fell into their hands?

Jes. Na! but when we heard that you were dying here, for want of Christian help, I cam' across to nurse ye.

Geor. My poor girl! But they will murder you; they show no mercy for age or sex.

Jes. I knaw it; here is the Calcutta news. It is fu' o' the bluidy wark the Nana Sahib made at Cawnpore.

Enter NANA.

Ee! talk o' the deevil——

Nana. Sahib, open your ears. Your countrymen are dogs. They still lie howling in the Residency—they dare not come forth—Inshallah——

Geor. They look for aid.

Nana. Their hearts lie, and hope will not feed them; their food is out, they cannot live on air.

Jes. Ye mistak'! they are living on an air noo, and is ca'd, "the Campbells are coomin'." And oh, could I but hear one screel of the pibroch—could I see the wavin' o' the bonnie tartan, and the braw line o' the shinin' steel, I'd na gie ye twa minits, but ye'd find the deevil before ye could say "Cawnpore."

Nana. Woman, be silent, read your printed words, and leave men to speak with men. [*To* GEORDIE.] Your countrymen are in our hands. Beneath this mosque, even below our feet, we have a mine, it passes beneath the fort commanded by the Sahib, your brother. Behold, the powder is laid, the match is ready; we can destroy him utterly, his fort once taken, the Residency is ours. Bismillah! have I defiled my tongue with lies?

Geor. The Rydan fort is the key to our position.

Nana. Enough blood has been shed—let him yield—his men shall go forth unharmed, we will pour the oil of mercy on their wounds.

Jes. [*Reading the paper.*] And under these conditions Cawnpore was surrendered ; the garrison marched out, and entered the boats provided for their safe transport.

Nana. You say your countrymen still look for aid, but they know not that the Sahib Havelock was defeated by my troops. From Lahore to Alahabad, Hindoostan is ours; you shall write these things that they may know ; they will believe your word, and they will yield. Inshallah! they shall go forth safely ; we will show mercy—on my head be it.

Jes. [*Reads.*] No sooner were the boats containing the troops, the women and children, in the midst of the stream than the enemy opened a murderous fire, and a work of slaughter began.

Nana. What woman is that? what writing has she in her hand? tear it away! [ACHMET *tears the paper from* JESSIE.] What says the pen there?

Jes. [*Rising.*] I'll tell ye in broad Scotch. It says that you have taught baith women and children to fecht, for you have found something that they fear more than death.

Ach. What's that?

Jes. The mercy of Nana Sahib!

Nana. Let my ferooshees come here.

Enter two Hindoos.

Take that woman and let her die.

Geor. Stay, Rajah, you would not kill that poor child.

[*At a signal from* ACHMET, *two cords descend from the roof.*]

Nana. You would have her life? Give me the letter to your brother ; she herself shall bear it to the Redan fort. [*They unbind* JESSIE.

Geor. That letter will not serve you. You do not know Randal McGregor—he will die, but will never yield.

Nana. Be it so. [*Rising.*] Achmet, hew away the right hands of these prisoners, and let their bodies swing from the heights of this mosque.

Ach. On my head be it.

Jes. Geordie, Geordie!

Geor. No, Nana, do not give me the death of a dog. Spare that poor child.

Nana. Stifle the howling of that hound.

Jes. Geordie, far'weel, Geordie!

Geor. Hold! what would you have me do?

Nana. [*Returning.*] Do you see yonder ropes? they ascend to the minaret of this mosque. [*To* ACHMET.] Prepare the means in yonder room to write. [*Exit* ACHMET.] Behold! write as I have said or give your neck to the cord. Choose—I have spoken.

Jes. Ay, but you have spoken to a McGregor!

[*They unbind* GEORDIE.

Re-enter ACHMET.

Geor. [*Aside.*] One day more—aid may come. Havelcck, Outram, cannot be far.

Jes. [*Aside.*] He hesitates—if he pens that letter a' is lost again, yet if I speak, the deevils will murder me.

Geor. [*Aside.*] She shall not die.

[*Enters,* R. H., *followed by* ACHMET. *Stage dark.*

Jes. [*Looking off,* R. H.] He will do't, to save my life, he will write down his infamy; nae if I bear it to the fort, I can tear it up on the way, but then they will kill him after a', and I ainly can be saved. Yonder he sits, he tak's the pen—his hand shakes, but still he writes, he writes, oh, what are the words? words of infamy, that will gae hame, and fill the faces of a' the Christian world wi' shame. Oh, could I reach his heart, I could stay his hand, but that black Beelzebub is wi' him. Eh! haud a wee, I'll speak to him. [*Sings.*

" Oh, why left I my hame," &c.

[*After first verse.*] He stops, his head fa's in his hand, tears, tears, he minds me, he minds me. [*She falls on her knees.*

[*She sings the 2nd verse.*]

He knows what I mean! [*A portion of the floor gives way, and falls in.* Ah! [*Starts back.*] What is that?

[*Cassidy puts his head through the orifice.*

Cas. Pooh! what a dust. Cheu! [*Sneezes.*] That was a big pinch of snuff anyway.

Jes. Wha's that? 'Tis Cassidy's voice.

Cas. I'll call Sweenie!

[*Sweenie's head appears through the orifice, beside Cassidy's.*

Jes. Sweenie!

Cas. Sweenie!

Sween. What's the matter?

Cas. Matther! Bedad there's an echo here that spakes first—a Hindoo echo that takes the words out av yer mouth.

Jes. Hush, 'tis I, Jessie.

Sween. Jessie!

Cas. Hoo! garry owen yer sowl! Hurroo!

Jes. Hush! gae down quick, they are coomin'.

[*Cassidy and Sweenie disappear, Jessie draws the nusmud or turkish carpet of the Divan over the orifice.*

Enter ACHMET *with a light.*

JESSIE *Sings,* " *My boy Tammie!* " *with affected unconcern.* ACHMET *examines the place, holds the light to her face, and goes out.* JESSIE *withdraws the carpet.*

Jes. Hush, silence, whesper. [SWEENIE *and* CASSIDY *re-appear.*

Cas. Where the divil are we at all.

Jes. This is a mosque, they ca' it. It is my prison and Geordie's. How did you get here?

Sween. We were working in the counter mine, ordered by the Captain, when we struck right into the mine, prepared by the rebels to blow us up, we removed their powder, of which we were running short, and then Cassidy and I took a stroll along their mine, to see the country.

Cas. The road was mighty dirty, but the view at the end of it, is worth the walk.

Jes. Then this passage goes under ground to the fort.

Cas. Bedad, Sweenie, we niver thought of that! it comes this way, but I don't know if it goes back the same.

Jes. D'ye see you ropes danglin' there, they are ready for me and Geordie. Twa hours mair, and ye'd been too late, down wi' ye noo, don't stir, until I tell ye.

Cas. We'll be as dumb as oysthers.

[*They disappear*, JESSIE *replaces the carpet.*

Re-enter the NANA. *Drums without.* *Re-enter* ACHMET. *Sepoys enter at back.*

Ach. A flag of truce from the fort.

Enter RANDAL *and* BLOUNT.

Jes. The McGregor!

Rand. You are the Nana?

Nana. I am he.

Rand. I command the Redan fort. I come to offer you an exchange of prisoners. We have taken sixty of your men.

Nana. They are in your hand, Inshallah! Mohammed Allah! Death is their portion. To each man his fate. [*Exit* ACHMET.

Rand. We fight our foes, we do not murder them.

Blount. Stay, Randal, don't be so fiery, let me speak to the Rajah. Salam, Aleikoom!

Nana. Allah, Resoul Allah! speak! There is no God but God, and Mohammed is his prophet.

Blount. There I can't agree with you, and I shall feel pleased to discuss that question at any time your leisure may permit. I am a minister of peace and a herald of mercy. Let me touch your heart. Our Heavenly Father, whom you call Allah, has given you rule and power over men; you have used it so cruelly, that all the world will shudder at your deeds of blood. This girl came here on a mission of mercy, she is not your prisoner; in every religion, and of all time, the weakness of woman protects her life, and makes her safety sacred.

Nana. The shepherds from the hills of the Himmelayah came to me and they said, Behold the tigers come out of the jungle and prey upon our flocks, and we fear. Which hearing, I arose; I sought the lair of the noble beast. I found there the tigress and her cubs. I slew them, until they died; and, lo, the tiger came, but did he whine and weep, saying, Sahib, you have done evil, my mate and my little ones are sacred, their weakness should protect them?

Blount. Are we tigers?

Nana. The tiger was placed here by Allah; he eats for his hunger, and kills that he may eat. Did Allah send the Briton here to make us slaves, to clutch us beneath his lion's paw, and to devour the land.

Inshallah! The voiceless word of God has swept over the people, and it says, Sufferers, arise, ye shall be free!

Ran. Freedom was never won by murder, for God has never armed the hand of an assassin.

Nana. What, dogs, are you to judge the ways of Allah?

Enter ACHMET *with a letter.*

Has the English prisoner written as I have said?

Ach. 'Tis done!

Jes. Na. it canna be!

Nana. The officer, your brother, knowing the folly of further resistance, writes here to you Sahib, and counsels you to yield.

Jes. Oh, I dar' na luk at Randal.

Rand. [*Striding up to* NANA.] You lie!

Blount. Randal, forbear, perhaps Geordie has been misled, deceived?

Rand. Deceit can make a man a fool, but not a coward.

Enter GEORDIE.

Geor. Randal!

Rand. Stand back! Lieutenant McGregor! the Rajah of Bithoor declares that in this letter to me, you have counseled to surrender. [*A pause.*] You are silent.

Geor. Randal, you will forgive me when you know all, but now and here, I dare not speak.

Nana. The proud brow of the Englishman, our tyrant, can be bowed down with shame. Achmet, read the letter.

Geor. No, no, not here.

Ach. I cannot; it's in a foreign tongue.

Blount. [*Looking over it.*] 'Tis in Gaelic, the native tongue of Scotland; I do not understand it.

Jes. Eh! I do; let me see. There's nae words in Gaelic that would serve a coward's tongue. Let me see. [*Music. She reads low.*] Eh, sirs, it is pure Gaelic, and rins so. [*To* NANA.] Open yer lugs, ye deevil, for here's porridge for ye, hotter than ye can sup it, maybe. [*Reads.*] To Captain Randal McGregor, Her Majesty's 78th Highlanders: My dearest brother, the Nana Sahib has doomed me to the death of a dog. My execution will take place at seven o'clock; you can spare our mother that grief, and me that disgrace. Jessie will point out to you the window of my prison—it looks over the Redan fort, and is within gun-shot of our men. As the clock strikes six, I will be at that window; draw out a firing party, and let them send three honest volleys through my heart. God bless you; give my love to Alice and Mary; remember me to all the fellows of our mess—let them give me a parting cheer when I fall. Your affectionate brother, Geordie McGregor.

Ran. Geordie, my brother! my own brother!

Geor. Randal!

Blount. [*Bursting into an ecstacy of delight.*] I can resist no longer. [*Shouts.*] God save the Queen!

[*Embraces* JESSIE. NANA *goes up with* ACHMET.

Ran. What guns are those?

Nana. My artillery cover the advance of the faithful on the Redan fort. Bind these men. Your hours are numbered.

Ran. Traitor! we are protected by a flag of truce.

Nana. Your flag of truce shall be your winding sheet. Swing their bodies, to the Minaret. As the hour strikes seven let it be done. [*The Hindoos seize* RANDAL, GEORDIE *and* JESSIE.] Let the old man go, that he may bear witness over all the earth, and strike white with terror the hearts of England, when they hear the vengeance of Nana Sahib. [*Exit.*

Blount. Don't! Hang me too, hang me! I'll be hung, if I die for it.

Ach. Slaves, see the Nana's order done, on your heads be it. On the stroke of seven, draw the ropes! my duty calls me to the mine. The mine below your countrymen. In five minutes the match will be lighted, and from above you will be able to see your soldiers blown to the skies.

[*Exit* ACHMET. *The Hindoos having bound* RANDAL, GEORDIE *and* JESSIE *exeunt.*

Jes. [*Calling.*] Sweenie, Cassidy, quick.

[CASSIDY *throws back the carpet.*

Cas. Here I am! [*Appears in the orifice.*] I'm nearly choked wid keepin' the fight in me. [*Jumps up.*

Blount. Where do you come from?

Cas. From the mine, alanna! Sweenie has run down below to look afther the naygur, that's gone to blow us up, he's got a word or two to say to him.

Ran. Quick, cut these cords, the executioners hold the other end, outside, and at the stroke of seven, they will run us up.

[CASSIDY *cuts the cords, aided by* BLOUNT.

Geor. Free! [*Embraces* JESSIE.

Sween. [*At the orifice.*] Come along, it's no use kicking.

Ran. Sweenie!

Sween. All right your honor. [*Salutes* RANDAL.] I've got a Hindoo Guy Fawkes, matches and lantern all complete.

Cas. Come up asy, darlint.

[SWEENIE *and* CASSIDY *pull* ACHMET, *gagged and bound, thro' the orifice.*

Ran. Secure that fellow, so that he may not give the alarm.

Cas. Never fear, Captain. [*Guns outside.*

Ran. The attack has commenced! To the Redan, Geordie, to the Redan. [GEORDIE *and* RANDAL *disappear down the orifice.*

Blount. Sweenie, spare that man, shed no blood boys, do you hear me.

Cas. All right, yer riverence.

Blount. Bind him fast, but let him live. [*He descends.*

Sween. Here is a rope, tie him with this.

[ACHMET *struggles and tries to speak, they throw him down.*

Cas. He's as lively as a cock salmon. Hould quiet ye divil, he's tryin' to spake.

Jes. [*Aside.*] That rope, they dinna ken what it is there for.

Cas. Tie him tight, and for fear he'd get the gag out and cry murdher, giv the rope a hitch round his neck.

Jes. Stop, release him, that cord is held by the executioners out-side, and at the stroke of seven. [*The great clock of the mosque strikes.*] Ah, mercy.

Cas. What is it?

[*The body of* ACHMET *is suddenly carried up, and disappears above through the roof.* CASSIDY *and* SWEENIE *look amazed.* JESSIE *utters a cry, and falls, hiding her face.*

END OF ACT II.

———•⬥•———

ACT III.

SCENE I.—*The Redan, a fort commanding a certain part of the City of Lucknow, and forming an outpost work, near the Residency. A breast work of gabions, fascines, and other military appliances embrace the stage. Through embrasures, four pieces of artillery are placed, one of them is dis-mounted, as if by a cannon ball. In the distance is seen the encampment of the rebel Sepoys, and three forts similarly constructed to the Redan, and mounted with artillery. The scene generally bears marks of a severe attack, both of musketry and cannonade. Groups of ladies with children, wounded soldiers, on guard, and some asleep.* CASSIDY *smoking a pipe, sits beside* JESSIE, *who is asleep, her head resting on his knapsack, and his grey coat spread over her.* SWEENIE, *with his head bound and wounded, leans on his musket.* MRS. CAMPBELL *and her two children on the* L. H., *a grey, cold light thrown over the scene, indicates the dawn of day.* GEORDIE *at the back is looking through a field glass, examining the position of the enemy.*

Mrs. C. Geordie, what can you see?

Geor. I can see the road to Alumbagh, from whence we expect re-lief, but there is no sign of troops there.

Mrs. C. Day after day we hope, until hope itself dies away—for three long months we have resisted.

Charlie. Mamma, I am hungry.

Mrs. C. God help you my poor child.

Geor. [*To the men.*] Lads, here's a little child starving, is there a crust among ye?

Sween. [*Saluting.*] Not a crumb, your honor, except it's in Phil Regan's kit, he died an hour ago. There he lies.   [*Points off,* R.

Geor. Search and see.   [*Exit* SWEENIE.

Enter RANDAL.

Rand. What news of the night?

Geor. Nine men dead of their wounds. Six gone into the hospital.

Rand. Inglis is hemmed in—can scarcely hold his own, like us, can scarcely sustain himself from hour to hour. If the columns of Gen-eral Havelock's force do not appear to-day, we must make Luck-now our permanent residence, Geordie.

Geor. You mean that you will die at this post?

[SWEENIE *re-enters with a morsel of bread, and hands it to* MRS. CAMPBELL. *She gives it to* CHARLIE, *who is going to eat it, but hesitates, breaks it in half and places one half of it in the hand of* EFFIE, *who still sleeps, then the child eats.*

Mrs. C. How is Jessie ? [GEORDIE *kneels beside* JESSIE.

Sween. She sleeps, but the long weeks of suffering has worn her spirit out at last.

Rand. Poor Jessie, has she too lost her spirits?

Cas. Lost her sperrits! Bedad, yer honor, the biggest keg of whiskey will give out at last if ye go dhrawin' at it ev'ry minit, an' afther Jessie cam' back, she tuk no rest, night or day, what wid nurse tendin' the woundid men, an' comfortin' the wimmin an' childer, an' cookin', an' kaping up the sperrit of the boys at the guns. When the hunger was in her mouth, she'd always have a song in id about the ould counthry that warrum'd our hearts, or a gay word to throw us in passin' that ud fetch the tear into our eyes. Lost her sperrits, Oh, achone! them sperrits was brewed in heaven above, they nivir touched the head but the heart of a man could get dhrunk upon 'em.

Mrs. C. Poor Jessie! she has been in a state of restless excitement through all the siege, and has fallen away visibly during the last few days. A constant fever consumes her, and her mind wanders occasionally, when recollections of home seem powerfully present to her. Overcome by fatigue, she has lain there since midnight, wrapped in her plaid. Poor child! it is strange, Randal, to see those rough men watch over her with the tenderness and grief of a mother over r a sick child.

Enter BLOUNT.

Blount. No news of relief?

Ran. None yet, but our fort here is cut off from the Residency, and Colonel Inglis may have dispatches.

Blount. Cheer up, lads, there's a good time coming. The old folks at home will long remember the defense of Lucknow, and every man here will be a hero in his own native village.

Cas. Except me, your riverence, divil native village I've got. I was born under a haystack, me father and mother had crossed to England for the harvest. Me mother died of me, and me father bruk his heart wid dhrinkin', so when they sent me home to Ireland, my relations would'nt own me, bekase I was an Englishman.

Blount. My good Cassidy, hearts like yours are never without a home, while there is goodness in earth and room in Heaven!

Cas. I'm content, sir! if Jessie was not sick, and I'd an ounce o' baccy, I would'nt call the Queen me uncle.

[*He draws the coat over Jessie.*

Geor. Here's the rations for the day.

[*Enter a Sergeant, with a tin vessel containing the food.*

Ran. Now, lads, there's no bugle to call ye to breakfast, so fall in and fall to. This is the last of our food, so make it go as far as you can. [*The food is divided amongst the men. They form a group and speak.*] As soon as the sun is up, we shall have warm work. So buckle your belts tight. [*A distant gun.*] There goes a how d'ye do from the rebels.

Sween. [*Advancing and saluting.*] Please your honor, the men wants to know very respectfully sir, please if this here ration is the last of our food, what's the children and ladies a' goin' to have sarved out.

Ran. That is a mutinous question, sir, fall in your ranks.

Sween. Ax your pardon, please sir—the men won't eat their rations till they know. They say they would'nt fight no how sir, anyways comfortable, if they ain't allowed to share all fair with the women and the little 'uns.

All the men. Share alike! Share alike!

Ran. Silence in the ranks! fall in, my good lads. Listen: for 80 days we have held this fort against fifty thousand rebels—from week to week our numbers have been thinned off, until we alone remain ; a few hours more, and General Havelock may arrive, [*a gun,*] but those few hours will be terrible. The rebel Sepoys grown desperate by repulse, will try to overwhelm us with their whole force. [*A gun.*] To preserve the loss of these weak ones, you must have strength to repel this attack. You are starving—the food you eat is their protection.

Sween. Please, Captain, the men say they'd feel worse after such a meal.

Ran. Do as you will, there is a Captain above who commands your hearts. Break ranks.

[*The men hasten to the various groups of women and children, and divide their rations with them.*

Blount. The Lord is with us. His spirit is amongst us ?

Geor. [*To* BLOUNT.] Will you not eat, sir ?   [*Offering him food.*

Blount. How can I, boy ? my heart is in my mouth, I have food enough in that. [*To the groups.*] Stay, my dear ones ! the food is poor, but let us not forget Him who gave it. [*Each person arrests his hand at the moment of eating.*] God bless us, and give us strength in this dark hour of our lives!   [*Jessie wakes.*

Jes. I'm cauld—I'm verra cauld.

Cas. Cowld, darlin ! sure it's September, and as hot as blazes—the Lord be praised.

Mrs. C. Jessie, are you better ?   [*Jessie looks round eagerly.*

Jes. I maun get my father's breakfast ; the gude man will be bock soon frae the field.

Cas. What is she talking about ?

Sween. Eat, Jessie dear—we have kept your ration till you awoke.

Jes. Eat! na—ah ! [*rejects the bread*] dinna ye see ? there's bluid upon it !

Cas. Blood !

Geor. Jessie !

Mrs. C. Jessie ? [*Crosses hastily to her.*] Jessie, you are ill. Look at me—speak to me—do you not know me ?   [*Kneels beside her.*

Jes. Knaw ye ! knaw ye ! Nae, but I ken a bonnie song—a song of Scotland—it's made o' heather and bluebells, woven in a tartan, and it is so gladsome that it maks me weep.

Mrs C. Randal, Randal, her senses have gone—her mind wanders.

Char. Jessie, my own Jessie! don't look so.

Jes. We'll gang hame. Coom to me—what's yer name?

Char. Charlie Fergus Campbell.

Jes. Then ye'ar Scotch—Scotch to the core of the heart. Listen.
[*Sings.*

" In winter, when the rain rained cauld," &c.

Sween. Jessie, Jessie dear? don't you know me? Sweenie.

Jes. Sweenie! where is he? He'll be outside the Byre, doon by the gates. After melkin the coos, I'll coom t'ye my lad. I'll steal away to the trystin, Sweenie. Fear nought. [*Sings.*

" Oh, whistle and I'll come to yer, my lad." &c.

Ran. Do not weep, Amy. She is happier so—and if we fail in repulsing the rebels to-day, or if we are not relieved by sundown, her madness will be a blessing—she will be insensible to her fate.

Mrs. C. Has the last hour come, Randal?
[*Three guns are heard in quick succession.*

Ran. Hark! the batteries are opening their fire. Fall in, men. Geordie, repel any advance by the left. I will hold the front.

Cas. [*Who has been looking over the back.*] Plase your honor, here come the black divils—they're upon us.

Ran. Steady men, no hurry.—Sweep them down.—Forward!
[*Exit* R.U.E. *with men.* MUSIC. *Exit* GEORDIE L. *with men. Sounds of musketry—cannon outside—drums.*

Blount. To your knees!—to your knees!—and pray!—this hour may be our last. Oh, if my scruples did not weigh so heavily upon me, I could strike for my country. [*Takes out a book.*

Jes. [*Who has been recovering her senses, as she listens to the conflict, at first with surprise, then with awakening comprehension.*] Ah! I mind it all—I am awak! where's Sweenie?

Blount. Let me read aloud to you, the words of peace and comfort. [*Jessie turns and sees the heads of some of the Sepoys at the embrasures, two of them are trying to escalade the breastwork.*] Look! look! they come!
[*The women utter a cry of dismay.*

Blount. The enemy! [*Pockets the book, and seizes a gun rammer.*] In the name of the Lord and of Gideon! [*He advances to the back.* The two wounded soldiers rise, and crawl to the guns. JESSIE runs to a bombshell, that lies, L. H., and finding CASSIDY'S pipe where he has thrown it still alight, she lights the fuse, and carries it with great difficulty to the breastwork, toppling it over. Blount standing on the disabled gun, deals ponderous blows right and left, with the rammer, and knocks over the Sepoys as they appear. The two wounded soldiers, JESSIE, ALICE and MRS. CAMPBELL, draw out the other gun, load it, and run it in again. The bomb is heard to explode outside, followed by cries and hurrahs. MRS. CAMPBELL applies a port fire to the gun, and fires it. Another shout. JESSIE leaps on the gun. The children bring hand grenades, and roll in a cannon ball. RANDAL and GEORDIE re-appear, R. and L., leading back their men, some wounded. Groups are formed. The ladies tear their dresses and make bandages for the wounded soldiers.*

Rand. Well done, bravely done! The enemy is repulsed, it was hot work.

Blount. Hot! It was terrible! I'm afraid I have killed somebody. I fear I have sent a sinner to his last account up there. [*Points up.*

Cas. [*Taking his arm and making him point it down.*] No, that's the way they wint. Bedad but ye made that shillelah dance like over their heads—they wint down by dozens—it was illegant.

Blount. I'll have to answer for this hereafter.

Cas. Oh, make yer mind asy! Damn the question ye'll ivir be axed about it.

Geor. Who sent that bomb, it fell into their advancing column and exploded with terrible effect?

Mrs. C. 'Twas Jessie.

Sween.
Cas.   }
Rand.   } Jessie!
Geor.

[*They look round,* JESSIE *is discovered crying bitterly, seated on the breastwork. They bring her forward.*

Mrs. C. Jessie, what ails you? why do you weep? [*To the rest.*] I never saw her cry before.

Alice. Dearest Jessie, are you wounded?

Jes. Na, na, but I canna help it. The clouds in my brain are pourin' oot, an'—an'—an—   [*Falls into hysterics.*

Alice. She is weak, poor child, hunger and fear have killed her.

Blount. No! this spasm of tears relieves her overburthened brain—she will recover.

Mrs. C. Leave her to Alice and me.

Char. Jessie, dear, don't 'ee cry, don't cry.
                              [JESSIE *embraces the children.*

Rand. [*Taking* BLOUNT *and* GEORDIE *aside.*] We have repulsed the first attack, but the enemy is too strong for us, they will try a second and a third—we have now only 20 men left—their next attack will succeed.

Blount. God's will be done. Let us thank Him that we are prepared to die. Yes, it is with joyful thankfulness that I say it. There is not one human being here, that has not shewn a noble, beautiful and Christian spirit, except me. I have been led away. The shepherd has killed his flock.

Rand. No, he has only driven the wolf away.

Blount. Let us hope that it may be forgiven me. Now what shall we do.

Geor. Alice, Amy, and Jessie, must they fall into the hands of these wretches? Oh, Randal, remember Cawnpore!

Blount. Let them decide. Let them know the worst, that they may prepare to meet their fearful fate.

Rand. I cannot speak it. I can face the enemy, but I cannot look into the pale faces of those women and tell them that my arm is powerless to defend their honor and their lives.

                    [*Goes up and seats himself dejectedly on a gun carriage.*

Blount. This is my mission. I will speak to them ; heaven inspires me with courage ! Geordie, tell me when the last moment is come. [*Sits,* R. H., *and takes out his book.*] Let me know when our death is near.

Mrs. C. Her temples throb and burn. My poor Jessie, lie down awhile and rest your head in my lap.

Geor. [*Near Blount.*] What are you reading ?

Blount. [*Looking up.*] The prayers for the dead !

[*Geordie goes up, and leans on the breastwork. The men are reposing in groups.*

Alice. How she trembles ! her hands are icy cold.

Mrs. C. Jessie, are you cold ?

Jes. [*Sings in a low voice.*]
  "In winter, when the rain rained cauld," &c.

Alice. Her senses wander again.

Mrs. C. Jessie, my dear Jessie ! try to rest your wearied brain—try to sleep.

Jes. Sleep ! Aye, let me sleep awee—but you will awak me when my father cooms frae the ploughin'.

Mrs. C. Yes, Jessie, when the gude man comes home, I will awake you. [*Aside.*] God help her !

Jes. I'm his ainly bairn, and he loos me well. [*Sings slowly the first few bars of "Robin Gray," as she falls to sleep.*

Geor. [*Advancing to Blount.*[The enemy are moving, sir—the time has come.

Blount. [*Closing the book.*] I am ready.
           [*Rises. Distant drum is heard, very low.*

Ran. The enemy ! Fall in, men !

[*Eight men rise, and form with Sweenie and Cassidy—Randal counts them.*

Ran. Ten ! ten men alone are fit for service—ten men to repulse a thousand !   [*Turns aside.*

Blount. My gentle friends—to you, weak in body but so strong in soul, I speak. It is fitting that you should know that the last hour has arrived. [*Drums. A gun.*] The last earthly hope is gone—let us address ourselves to heaven.

Alice. Will these men desert us ?

Blount. In an hour not one of those men will be living.

Mrs. C. But we shall be living. Oh, recollect Cawnpore ! these children will be hacked to pieces before our eyes—ourselves reserved for worse than death, and then mutilated, tortured, butchered in cold blood. Randal, will you see this done—will you not preserve us from this fate.   [*Alice weeps on Geordie's breast.*

Ran. Amy, my heart is broken. What can we do ?

Mrs. C. Kill us. Put us to a merciful death ere you fall. Oh, Randal, do not turn away from me—think of the fate reserved for her you love. Oh, death, death ! a thousand times death ! You are going to die—take us with you, Randal ; if you leave us here, you are accessories to our dishonor and our murder.

Blount. They come, they come—already they begin to ascend the hill.

Alice. Geordie.

Mrs. C. Quick, or it will be too late. Quick, Randal—oh, remember we are cowards—we are women and we may not have the courage to kill ourselves.

Ran. I cannot, Amy, I cannot.

Mrs. C. Lend me your dirk, then. Rather than see my children mutilated, tortured, they shall die. God will forgive a mother when her children plead for her.

Blount. They are here, Randal—they are here.

Ran. Murderers! they come for their prey. [*Dashing down his bonnet.*] Yes, I will tear it from their rage. Soldiers, one volley—your last—to free your countrywomen from the clutches of the demons. One volley to their noble and true hearts, and then give your steel to the enemy. Load.

[*The soldiers bite off the ends of their cartridges and load their muskets. The women cast themselves into each other's arms and form a group.*

Blount. [*Begins to read the service for the dead.*] In the midst of life we are in death.

[*A distant wail of the bagpipes is heard.* JESSIE *starts from her sleep.*

Ran. Shoulder arms. Ready!

[*Another wail of the pipes is heard.*

Jes. Ah! [*Utters a cry.*] Hark—hark—dinna ye hear it? dinna ye hear it? Ay! I'm no dreamin', it's the slogan of the Highlanders! we're saved—we're saved! [*Throws herself on her knees.*] Oh, thank God! whose mercy never fails the strong in heart, and those that trust in him.

Ran. Relief! no! it is impossible!   [*Guns outside.*

Jes. I heard it! I heard it!

Geor. Here comes the enemy!

Jes. To the guns, men, to the guns! Courage! Hark! to the slogan. 'Tis the slogan of the McGregor, the grandest of them a'. There's help at last. Help! d'ye hear me? help!

Ran. There is no signal from the Residency. Jessie, your ears deceive you.

Mrs. C. She is mad!

Jes. I am not daft, my Scotch ears can hear it far awa'. [*Bagpipes sound nearer.*] There again—there—will ye believe it noo—d'ye hear —d'ye hear? the Campbells are comin'!

[*The Bagpipes swell out louder, but still distant. Distant musketry is heard to roll. Shouts!*

Geor. See, the flag runs up at the Residency. 'Tis true.

                                                        [*Cannonade.*

Ran. To arms! men! One charge more, and this time drive your steel down the throats of the murderous foe.   [*Musketry.*

Jes. Ha! they coom! they coom! yonder is the tartan. Oh! the bonnie Highland plaid. [*She waives her tartan plaid.*] You have nae forgotten us.

[*The pipes here change the air to " Should Auld Acquaintance be Forgot."*

D'ye hear! d'ye hear, "Should Auld Acquaintance be Forgot," noo lads, here come the rebels. It will be yer last chance at them.

[*She leaps down.*

Ran. Steady lads!   [*The Sepoys appear at the back.*
All. Hurrah!

[*They dash up the breast work and after firing, club their guns and disappear fighting, driving the Sepoys down. Shouts and musketry and cannonade, grow furious. The back scene is covered with a red glow; explosions, as from mines, are heard, through all of which the bagpipes continues, now very loud and near. The Hindoos appear fighting, and driven in at the back. They fall over the breast work;* RANDAL *and the Highlanders, with their piper, charge up the breastwork and crown it in every direction, bearing down the Sepoys with the bayonet.* GEORDIE *and his men enter* L. H. CASSIDY *and* SWEENIE *from* R. H., *with others of the men, face those of the Sepoys, who are driven over by the Highlanders.*

TABLEAU.

———— • ◁▷ • ————

NOTE FROM THE AUTHOR.—The powerful incident with which this drama concludes, incited me to construct the domestic fiction contained in the first and second acts. Its dramatic value I had seen tested by Mr. Everett, on an audience at the Academy of Music, rendered breathless and hysterical by the sweet power of his pathetic description. Yet the task of dramatising the subject might have been abandoned had I not possessed, in my own wife, a representative for the character of Jessie Brown, singularly adapted to its realization. Her Scottish blood warmed to the subject; her Scotch dialect, and her power of delineating Highland character, assured me that the central figure of my dramatic group would be faithfully rendered. I hope that in the treatment of this pretty subject, the reader may find I have not injured the beautiful sentiment of the original tale.

DION BOURCICAULT.

THE following account is taken from the letters of a lady, one of the rescued on the 26th September, when Lucknow was relieved by the forces under Sir Colin Campbell:

"Death stared us in the face. We were fully persuaded that in twenty-four hours all would be over. The engineers had said so, and all knew the worst. We women strove to encourage each other, and to perform the light duties which had been assigned to us, such as conveying orders to the batteries and supplying the men with provisions, especially cups of coffee, which we prepared day and night. I had gone out to try and make myself useful, in company with Jessie Brown. Poor Jessie had been in a state of restless excitement all through the siege, and had fallen away visibly within the last few days. A constant fever consumed her, and her mind wandered occasionally, especially on that day, when the recollections of home seemed powerfully present to her. At last, overcome with fatigue, she lay down on the ground, wrapped up in her plaid. I sat beside her, promising to awaken her when, as she said, "her father should return from the ploughing." She at length fell into a profound slumber, motionless and apparently breathless, her head resting in my lap. I myself could no longer resist the inclination to sleep, in spite of the continual roar of cannon. Suddenly I was aroused by a wild, unearthly scream close to my ear ; my companion stood upright beside me, her arms raised and her head bent forward in the attitude of listening. A look of intense delight broke over her countenance, she grasped my hand, drew me towards her, and exclaimed, "Dinna ye hear it? dinna ye hear it? Ay, I'm no dreamin'; its the slogan o' the Highlanders! We're saved, we're saved!" Then, flinging herself on her knees, she thanked God with passionate fervor. I felt utterly bewildered; my English ears heard only the roar of artillery, and I thought my poor Jessie was still raving, but she darted to the batteries, and I heard her cry incessantly to the men, "Courage! hark to the slogan—to the Macgregor, the grandest of them a'! Here's help at last." To describe the effect of these words upon the soldiers would be impossible. For a moment they ceased firing, and every soul listened in intense anxiety. Gradually, however, there arose a murmur of bitter disappointment, and the wailing of the women who had flocked out began anew as the Colonel shook his head. Our dull lowland ears heard nothing but the rattle of the musketry. A few moments more of this deathlike suspense, of this agonising hope, and Jessie, who had again sunk on the ground, sprang to her feet, and cried in a voice so clear and piercing that it was heard along the whole line—"Will ye no believe it noo? The slogan has ceased, indeed, but the Campbells are comin'. D'ye hear, d'ye hear?" At that moment we seemed indeed to hear the voice of God in the distance, for now there was no longer any doubt of the fact. That shrill, penetrating, ceaseless sound, which rose above all other sounds, would come neither from the advance of the enemy nor from the work of the Sappers. No, it was indeed the blast of the Scottish bagpipes, now shrill and harsh, as threatening vengeance on the foe, then in softer tones, seeming to promise succor to their friends in need. Never surely was there such a scene as that which followed. Not a heart in the Residency of Lucknow but bowed itself before God. All, by one simultaneous impulse, fell upon their knees, and nothing was heard but bursting sobs and the murmured voice of prayer. Then all arose, and there rang out from a thousand lips a great shout of joy which resounded far and wide, and lent new vigor to that blessed bagpipe. To our cheer of "God save the Queen!" they replied in the well-known strain that moves every Scot to tears." Should auld acquaintance be forgot," &c. After that nothing else made any impression on me. I scarcely remember what followed."

THE END.